A NOTE TO PARENTS

Early Step into Reading Books are designed for preschoolers and kindergartners who are just getting ready to read. The words are easy, the type is big, and the stories are packed with rhyme, rhythm, and repetition.

We suggest that you read this book to your child the first few times, pointing to each word as you go. Soon your child will start saying the words with you. And before long, he or she will try to read the story alone. Don't be surprised if your child uses the pictures to figure out the text— that's what they're there for! The important thing is to develop your child's confidence—and to show your child that reading is fun.

www.randomhouse.com/kids/

Library of Congress Cataloging-in-Publication Data
Corey, Shana. Babe : oops, pig! / by Shana Corey ; illustrated by Donald Cook ; based on characters created by Dick King-Smith. p. cm. — (Early step into reading)
SUMMARY: Babe the pig gets into mischief when he tries to help out with chores on the farm.
ISBN 0-679-88967-1 (pbk.) — ISBN 0-679-98967-6 (lib. bdg.)
[1. Pigs—Fiction. 2. Farm life—Fiction.] I. Cook, Donald, ill. II. Title. III. Series.
PZ7.C8155Bad 1998 [E]—dc21 97-40800

Printed in the United States of America 10 9 8 7 6 5 4 3 2 1

EARLY STEP INTO READING is a trademark of Random House, Inc.

Early Step into Reading™

BABE
The Sheep Pig™

Oops, Pig!

By Shana Corey

Illustrated by Donald Cook

Based on characters created by Dick King-Smith

Random House 🏠 New York

The sun comes up.
"Quack-a-doodle-doo!"
shouts the duck.

Babe is still asleep.

Wake up, sleepyhead!

Time for breakfast!

Pancakes for the farmer.

Hay for the horses.

Feed for the chickens.

And slop for Babe!

Time for chores.

Gather the eggs, Babe.

Milk the cow, Babe.

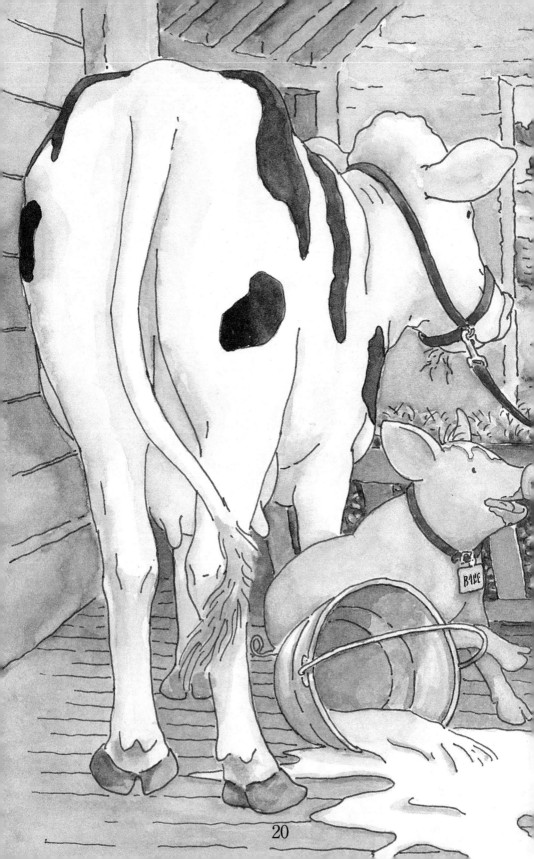

Weed the garden, Babe.

Oh, dear!

"Babe! What a mess
you have made!"

Babe wants to help.

What can he do?

Babe can herd sheep!

"Good job, Pig,"
says the farmer.